THE LIBRARY OF THOMAS RIVKA

MARTIN NAKELL

The Library of Thomas Rivka

NEW AMERICAN FICTION
SERIES: 40

SUN & MOON PRESS
LOS ANGELES • 1997

Sun & Moon Press
A Program of The Contemporary Arts Educational Project, Inc.
a nonprofit corporation
6026 Wilshire Boulevard, Los Angeles, California 90036

This edition first published in paperback in 1997 by Sun & Moon Press
10 9 8 7 6 5 4 3 2 1
FIRST EDITION

This book was made possible, in part, through a matching grant from
the California Arts Council and through contributions to
The Contemporary Arts Educational Project, Inc.,
a nonprofit corporation

Cover: André Kertesz, *Mondrian's Studio* (1926)
Design: Katie Messborn
Typography: Guy Bennett

LIBRARY OF CONGRESS CATALOGING IN PUBLICATION DATA
Nakell, Martin [1945]
The Library of Thomas Rivka
p. cm—(New American Fiction Series: 40)
ISBN: 1-55713-089-2 (alk. paper)
I. Title. II. Series.
PS3564.A5314L53 1997
813'.54—dc21
97-14755 CIP

Printed in the United States of America on acid-free paper.

for Jessica, Stacy & Joren

I / The Construction of Infinity

The wall emerges from a point on the ground which for mathematical and architectural and literary purposes let's agree to call zero. From zero the wall rises gradually along the one architectural/geometric/draftsman's line of infinity, that line which has no natural destination or deflection, which describes the possibility of infinitude upward. Compare this to a spiral. We imagine no end to a spiral. Theoretically, a spiral can go on turning around itself, and then opening to the next level of its not quite repetitive evolution as long as there is material to build with. But even a spiral we imagine as capable of expanding to a certain point only, and then losing strength, dissipating, *dissipare,* disappearing. A line maintains its energy at every point.

As any event occurs we fix it in time and simultaneously give it the timelessness which is the redeeming and sensuous nature of memory. So does the wall gain both existence and its opposite, infinity, in the very same act of being, at each and every fictional point along its continuum.

Yet because the wall's line emerges from zero, we imagine that line also continues in the opposite direction, through zero, down into some mirror world we can conceive, but can't make known.

The wall is a light grey stucco, textured, so that if you ran your hand along it you'd feel its bumps, as if infinity were made palpable. The wall seems to stand very still inside the westerly wing of Thomas's house, having achieved intricate balance and value among chaotic forces: vector, gravity, tension, isometry, dissonance, G force. A balance held by counter-weight against its anti-world?

Along this wall Thomas Rivka, over many years, has built his library. He works here as much as he can find time for. Sometimes at the desk he's set up in the open area near the large south-facing window. But often Thomas will sit on the red tile stairs which ascend along the wall, especially if he's perusing. Thomas Rivka is an eclectic reader. He follows one clue into another. Sitting on the steps suits him because he can look over a book or two from one section of the library, decide not to read it just now and move on.

Thomas tried to establish guidelines for filling the library. Was there any exigency outside of his own taste for building such a library? Could the library have an urgency of its own which superseded Thomas's whims? Should he keep books that he didn't like? Should he keep a book he didn't like by someone he knew? Should he keep a book he didn't like by someone he knew, whom he didn't like? Should he keep a book which might be—to a librarian, say, or a historian—an important book, but which to him was a boor? Should he save room? Should he try to achieve some kind of completion? Should he organize the library in a simple author by author alphabet, or by some other system which the library itself demanded? Thomas's books stood in boxes, unusable. When he finally began to unpack them he'd spent enough time in the new, shelf-empty library to know that it had no requirements of its own. It left him free to do whatever he wanted. What he wanted was to have no policies, to let each book be a unique decision, with the hope that some shape would emerge. Then even if he was too close to the thing to see that shape, he might at least sense it.

Thomas has read some of the books several times. Some he's never read. So the process of reading in this infinite library of the infinite wall isn't limited by the number of books. One book could make such a library. Of course, Thomas Rivka's library is lacking thousands, surely millions of books, including those not yet written, including this one. He imagines as he reads that the possibilities of potential books are contained in the reality of extant books.

No past reading can be recaptured or relived except as memory because every alphabet moves in one direction or another. Every time Thomas comes to read is a different time because he arrives with the additional knowledge and experience of his last reading. In fact, you might say, because each time is new, that Thomas has never read anything until today, that until now he's been preparing to read, and that today, as he reads for the first time, it's an astonishing event for him. But for us also who watch Thomas Rivka because we, who have also never read anything yet, anticipate the time in the not too distant future when we'll go to our own first reading, bringing to it the full zero of our experience by which we might have some context for understanding. Or that moment might be right now, as we read this. In fact, this might be the only opportunity there is for such a moment.

II / The Defining of Zero

On December 31st Thomas woke up in the dark just before dawn. He showered and dressed quietly, not to wake his wife, then went to the library with the idea in mind of reading from de Gomara's *Cortes*. He'd woken up sickened by a dream of being run down, hunted, chased and attacked, but unable to defend himself. He wanted to read about—and especially to look at—pictures of the battle of Tenochtitlan, as if he could draw some primary strength from the madness of a warrior like Cortes, whose medieval motto was *Judicium Domini apprehendit eos, et fortitudo ejus correboravit bracchium meum.** Thomas didn't believe in any Deus Domini Elohim, or in any god, but he believed in certain primary forces in the world. After the defeat in his dream left him pale he hoped to ingest some of that brutal elan from the warrior Cortes.

When he got to the library all the books were gone. This was no hallucination. And it was no dream. And it was no literary metaphor. He ran the palm of his hand along the clean emptiness of bare shelves as he climbed each stair to the top.

* The Judgement of the Lord overtook them; His might strengthened my arm.

Thomas sat on the top step, beside the small square window set back into the wall. Snow covered everything in the windless cold. He looked back down the staircase.

There might be a euphoria to these empty shelves. A freedom of freshness. But Thomas was long past his ability to believe in those kinds of delusions. He knew that whatever freedom he had on this earth came from a continuous engagement with the same things and people and ideas and problems and activities over and over. Newness was only there in repetition if ever, which he reminded himself of from time to time by reading Heraclitus. Christ! The Heraclitus was gone. And the *Cortes*. Those books had his notes in them. They'd been bought in memorable places on certain memorable occasions. The *Cortes*, for example. He'd bought that the very day after the new American President George Bush had given his first speech to the American Congress and the nation. That speech was a retrenchment of the presidency, rescuing it from the nation's dalliance with Hollywood glitzy illusion and returning it to faith in the substantially wealthy, white, honest Protestant rule of noblesse oblige which hid its savagery so effectively in the language of moderation and good sense. President Bush told the country that he had campaigned as the Education President, and—pounding the podium which held his carefully arranged words—he *would be* America's Education President. The next day the *New York Times* published the details of the President's new budget, including his cut of three billion dollars from education spending, which in any case was .148 percent of the defense budget. Thomas had been in town that day, read the

Times, bought the de Gomara, and was enthralled by at least the honest sword of the outright imperialist conqueror Cortes.

Each book in the library had some mark. The autographed *Absalom, Absalom.* The 1822 *Paradise Lost* bought in London. The Greek Homer brought by Anastasios from Thessaloniki. The Hebrew Artaud. Each thought was a panic. Bits of his own body, certainly of his mind, almost of his memory.

Khlum scratched at the door. Thomas took her out and walked with her in the woods. He hunted for some meaning to the disappearance of the library. Hadn't he been too dependent on the books? Wasn't he missing out on other things because he spent too much time reading? Were the books leading him astray in some way, their disappearance a warning from Plato's *Republic,* Cervantes's *Quixote*? Was he too proud of the library? Had he just taken it for granted? These questions were all so egocentric, and all presuming some moral lesson at the core of this event.

But to begin again? From a beginning dispossessed? To put one single book on those hollow shelves. Then a second. A third. During the next few months Thomas remembered almost every book. Even ones he hadn't read he remembered as though he knew them well: expectation itself is a kind of bond. He remembered covers, bindings, notes which came from some irrecuperable moment of response whose importance was entwined with Thomas's life at that moment and no other. As he read he wrote his own book: The Readings of Thomas Rivka, by Thomas Rivka.

Thomas walked past the empty library every day, climbed the stairs, considered the curve of infinity and the problem of zero. Was zero emptiness, negation? But if so of what kind: the emptiness of potential actuality always potential? Fecund emptiness? Or banal, dead emptiness, desolate, ashen, the emptiness of some deserted urban scene where there are only buildings crowded in on themselves and garbage in the streets and a hot sun and still air? White (reflective, rejective) or black (receptive, inclusive) emptiness? Could he say that zero existed as some series of moments in time? As a kinetic moment that was part of kinetic time that he was also either part of or not part of? Was zero the movement of time itself measured by zero per zero? The movement of books? Or did it actually exist in some other, alternative dimension, some other possible universe? The books, he even speculated, had gone on to that other library that began in that other universe that extended out in the other direction through the zero on the floor where the wall began. The Invisible Library of Thomas Rivka. Hah! There should be invisible books there, he argued, negative books, other-universe books whose language Thomas couldn't ever read, a language maybe altogether independent of the signified.

But zero wasn't a philosophical idea. It was practical mechanics, a Mayan tool, a fictional cornerstone to a real world (like the passive verb *to be*), necessary to arithmetic and so necessary to planting, building, keeping records of transactions, counting populations, keeping debts in order, harvesting food, moving earth from here to there. Zero was the catalyst in everything, visible everywhere.

Thomas's conclusion from all this was that in any case zero's relationship to the disappearance of his library was inconclusive, if related. So multifaceted it could be thought about forever. Yes.

His wits were dulled by not reading. His thoughts were more contained in a smaller world with fewer connections. He began to recite what he remembered of certain books by heart, or just to tell their stories or arguments or histories or ideas to other people, to deliver whole discourses and recitations to Malka, to Eddy, to his father. They were mostly enthralled and it was a pleasure for them. Thomas knew this was how books had begun, as oral recitations, and it excited him as he began to understand the impulse at the heart of the origins of culture. He used ancient memory techniques: repetition and kenning, trying as much as he could to stay true to the originals. He tried to invent a few tales himself, but he wasn't a writer and he was satisfied that he was no more an oral writer than he was a literate writer.

On May 25, exactly 6 days short of five months of the morning Thomas discovered the books missing, he arose very early, just before dawn, showered and dressed, and walked past the library. A violent, vivid dream again had left him feeling uncomfortable and he wanted to walk outside before breakfast to shake off its effects. All the books were returned. Shelved. Arranged.

Thomas stopped at the foot of the wall. He looked up at the shelves. Each book was in its place. "Where have you been? Where?" The books sat as they always had. "You're intractable," he said to them, but they didn't agree or disagree. Thomas paced off excited energy. "I'll tell you," he said, "I'm no longer your slave." They didn't answer. "You no longer have such power over me." Their silence. "You're no longer the main gate to my solitude."

"Why?" Thomas asked. "Answer me somehow, please. One very simple question I've been haunted by for nearly five months: why?" The books didn't even suggest that they contained an answer he might hunt out in them. In fact they suggested there was no answer for him to search for. Their presence seemed to suggest, if anything, that they had returned, and Thomas might go on with his reading, if he wanted to.

Thomas sat on the twenty-third stair, the very middle, with his feet on the twenty-first stair, his eyes shifting among the hundreds of familiar titles. Then he climbed to the top and looked out the window. The fields were green and the air lightly blue. He decided to go out walking, then come back and read for a while before breakfast. The return of the books was certainly not a metaphor for the return of color to the fields. They could have gone in summer and come back in winter, on December thirty-first, and not have been a metaphor for the birth of Christ or the turning of the year or the hacking up of some god/king and the planting of his body in the four corners of antiquity. What kind of ritual is it to read? Or what kind of act?

Wasn't it the *History and Conquest of Mexico and Peru* he'd meant to read when the books disappeared? Who was it chasing him in that dream? Who is his enemy?

III / The Poetics of Thomas Rivka

: theirs the
languages flickering
always I or an I   who's about to utter
: those books
other languages we've been speaking
another tangent of
about whose convergence

that no book has ever given me courage
or that no book has taught me anything I didn't already know
that no book has talked about anything I hadn't already imagined
no book that has answered an important question
yet lasts longer than our memory of it
no book has contained more mirrors than history more frames
and that no book still looking has found a way to circumvent the numbering of pages or trick us
into disbelieving time for longer than some time
books contradicting each other propelling history
a necessity

no book has caused me to kill anyone
and that no book has caused me not to kill
I would like to say that each book has looked at me

that books both are and are not ciphers
redolent themselves of any given zero

if the books communicate with each other

I mean in our absence
I mean in a significant way
Means adding or detracting from

Heschel's God in search of mankind
and books without their jealousy waging wars
an eruptive library not in search in possession of

books whose whole conceptions are whole
whose absences included

or what potential eyes might do with those few
                                                                contemporary
poems
stones   absorbent of instabilities

themselves in flux

sun: our revolutions/night: its
repetitive patterned its light across libraries
changing the contents
because repetitive
subjunctive patterned

potential eyes.
Reading my reading.

that I have never given books courage

in her garden.
On my way to the library reading about root seed soil cul-
tivation bloodworm bacilli virus   root   cure.
her many questions in a rising syllable.

preparing the ground she's perfectly tired,
perfectly worried and has a perfect ignorance
of our English language.
Chinese, maybe.

It's important to tell her everything I've read
because she's so carefully listening to me each word
she waits for me to get to the book
which contains her
an elderly Chinese neighbor
works in the garden has always worked, and to tell her
about it
so she can see it, garden and all, as though it were news,
some clear phenomena

Chinese, perhaps.
each word
capacities for syntax
long narratives, stories full of birds
and not just to pass the time

As the pages are turned their transparency, along with their dimensions

The letters, which are also raised, also transparent, and also their dimensions

The persons turning the enormous pages, three of them, masters of their craft, devoted, limited in scope

Larger than a Book of Kells, much larger than those in the libraries at Nineveh or Monte Cassino or South Pasadena

The pages moving at the set speed

Because a certain delight in watching the Lilliputian page turners, a kind of giddiness, yet wanting to discern the text in the pages passing quickly

Their skill. Their adroitness. Their agility. Your laughter. An encroaching recognition of indiscernability.

Prior to the time when understanding closed in on things?

Or later, a wistfulness that the pages couldn't have been read? An anger?

An agreement among everyone, and you too had to agree, given the alternative.

Not memory, but image, of pages unread

Their delight, not in your ignorance, although that is a consequence

Given that there is no such time as prior to
Or if there is no such time as prior to

not to confuse memory
with reading if the difference

who have banned or tried to ban certain reading at certain times:

the Los Angeles County Museum of Art, the Roman Grand Consul, John Milton, the New York Society for the Suppression of Vice, Samuel Roth, the Archdiocese of Lintang, Taiwan, The Council of Sens, the United States Espionage Act of 1917, the Council of Ephesus, Les

Jeunesses Patriotiques, the Roman Index, the Tridentine Index, the Index of Pius IV, the Index of Benedict XIV, the British Home Office, the United States Supreme Court, the City of Cleveland, Ohio, the Roman Inquisition, the Emperor Charles V, the Imperial Diet of Nuremberg, the Synod at Cologne, the Paris Police, the Ministry of Propaganda and Popular Enlightenment of the Third Reich, Czar Nicholas I, Czar Alexander III, Les Camelots du Roi, Chancellor Metternich, The Reich Press Chamber, the South African Government, the National Vigilance Association, the United States Sedition Act, Ferdinand and Isabella, The National Endowment for the Arts, the Government of Francisco Franco, the City of El Viejo, California, my grandmother, the Greek philosopher Thadaïses, the monks of the Abbey Lepanto in the canonization of the Bible a pin with which to prick

the air continuously in motion

  a shovel to dig, a tool micro or macro
      to discover an imperfect cipher
      unround, a-rooted
beginnings and endings crossed
while history stands revealed
brutal as unrepentant as necessity

within certain texts
that certain despair(s)
in recurrence
in hopeful constancy

the word stone
because it's the first thing, stone
or the last   (ing)
or neither first nor last
but is one of those words

IV / The Discourses on Reading

Reading Hamlet, you pull down a book that summarizes the history of Hamlet criticism. It describes the Romantic theory that Hamlet had failed to act swiftly because he was too much bound up in thought; the psychoanalytic theories that for Hamlet to kill Claudius would be to commit Oedipal murder, an act so terrifying as to cause any young prince good pause; the existential theory that action in an absurd world is so questionable that it's an enormous task just to muster the effort to overcome the inertia of meaninglessness. The deconstructive reading that suggests Hamlet didn't fail to act at all, that for Hamlet, delay was no more right or wrong than action would have been. Among all these theories you wonder: Did Hamlet fail to act? You toss the theories against each other. You enter each theory and pursue it but each time you're left wandering, turning from one irresolute, contradicted direction to another. Look at the play's beginning, for example. When Horatio tells Hamlet about the ghost's appearance on the ramparts Hamlet doesn't hesitate. "I would I had been there," and later that very night he goes there. When the ghost appears and beckons Hamlet—possibly to death, to torment, to hell—Hamlets says, "What should be the fear?...It waves me forth again. I'll follow it."

The multitude of theories begin to fold in on each other so that walking the top of one your head brushes against the bottom of another. But you feel determined to find some answer for yourself. Then it seems it wasn't the answer to Hamlet you were trying to pin down, but to some other question, some other quest. Lost in these pursuits, you turn one last corner in the maze of critique and your foot, before you instructed it to step or not to step, has stepped off over an edge and you are tumbling: your wits abandon you and it becomes clear in the chaos that all your life you had read for one reason, and that your library had one purpose. As a young boy—by following the path of one book to the next—you'd come to believe that by reading you would eventually, finally come to turn the key in the most arcane or imaginary nodule of consciousness and the world would be reversed, the grit of its daily clothes would fall away and it would be revealed as it really was: clear and eternally new. Not compromised at all, not corrupt, not dim.

At first you berate yourself for carrying such a desire far into adulthood, for failing to recognize it until now, for having built a major part of your life around an unrecognized motive. Hadn't you learned long ago that life was the ability to immerse yourself in the corrupt world, relinquishing yourself to the unrevealed presence of daily life? Hadn't you known that?

To steady the spinning in the moment of your recognition you look at the inner spine of the book. No matter how much experience you imbibe hopping from book to book you will never turn the page to reveal that world.

And even *that* recognition will not unlock that distant nodule of consciousness.

All your life you've read to discover something. What you've discovered is that you'll not discover it. So.

It reminds you of a story you read in a collection of mystical tales. A Jewish story, 15th Century, if you remember correctly. It was about Rabbi Ahdam, and his son, BenAhdam. When Rabbi Ahdam died he had to transmit his knowledge, in the form of a book (typical Jewish tale), to a worthy successor, someone strong enough to digest its mysteries. He knew that his son, BenAhdam, wasn't that person. So he gave the book to BenAhdam with instructions to deliver it to an obscure poor boy, a boy who served anonymously in a distant synagogue. Rabbi Ahdam had observed the boy, Koach, and seen the spark of the mystical fire burning in him, that spark which ignites the thirst which can't be quenched.

Following these directions, BenAhdam took his father's book to the young Koach, who grew into it, BenAhdam serving as Koach's servant for many years. Finally BenAhdam couldn't stand it anymore. As though his birthright had been stolen from him, he had to peer into the secrets for himself. He pressured Koach to take him on the journey.

Koach relented, and they began the long process with a cleansing fast (typical mysticism). As things progressed, as days and nights went by, the arduous process overwhelmed BenAhdam. His father had been right. BenAhdam wasn't strong enough. In the middle of a night of vigilance when it was essential not to drop off into sleep, BenAhdam gave in to both his physical weariness and his emotional limitations. He lost his attention. He opened himself and his drowsiness grew into him. He slept, and because he slept, he died.

What a character! BenAhdam. Did he only imagine there were great spiritual secrets? But there you go again, already off into a story as though you were reading. In pursuit of something. As though nothing had happened this morning.

Now you know you will go on reading. You will go on filling these shelves in what logically seems now like perverse activity. But you know that doesn't prove that it is perverse: it only proves the perverse element in logic, it forces you to find some resolve beyond reason, if resolve is not itself a quality of reason, in which case you are forced to find both resolve and logic beyond reason.

Was there an aspect of the tragic in all this? Are you after all any kind of Hamlet? Who was Hamlet? That's the interesting thing. Were you merely footman in your library of unrevealed disquisitions, voices lost talking to each other? Do you think too much?

The book of Hamlet criticism was by an Irish scholar: Joyce Joyce, reputed to be the wife of the grand-nephew of James Joyce, and it was James Joyce who said that Hamlet was Leopold Bloom, or Stephen Dedalus. Or wasn't it that Hamlet was the ghost of Shakespeare's father? You'll have to go back to that chapter in Ulysses and look it up and re-read Joyce's meanderings. But later.

You put the Joyce Joyce book down and go back to

where you'd left off in Hamlet: III.2, where Hamlet complains to Rosencrantz & Guildenstern who would presume to discover Hamlet's problem, and Hamlet says to them: "You would play upon me, you would seem to know my stops, you would pluck out the heart of my mystery."

You think about naming your library: The Library of Rosencrantz and Guildenstern. Or the Library of BenAhdam, not because BenAhdam failed, but because he intuited that imbedded in the fiber and ink of the pages of the book there was some awareness about to be realized, very nearly known.

V / Apologia Epistolarium

Dear Jake W.,

Because what we read has almost happened, while what we live exists as a flickering. No matter how much we stare we can't make reality even as real as the eyes that are staring. Because. Because everyday life envies the library, that's why. Everyday life attacks the library. Would destroy it. It's not paranoia it's science. The acid in the air eats at the substance which contains the clues to the languages of the author/reader. The salt in the air digs into the covers, into the bindings. In summer dry air absorbs the books' moistures, dries out their glues, turns them into withered visages. In winter cold air has a go at it. Think of newspapers. They dry up quickly because the paper is cheap, but the paper is cheap because the imaginative life of the newspaper is minimal. News is quick. I have shelves full of Ozymandiases, of sphinxes, but it isn't only the elements and their raw conspiracy with time which eats at these very-much-less-than-monuments, it's even more the envy of everyday life. That's the harsh acid. Everyday life which is so hungry for the imagination these books possess, for that quality that occurs between reader and writer, reader and text, text and text.

What is it that goes on here that's so different from everyday life? So alluring to it that everyday life uses the weapons of nature to destroy the claim this library has on a life, on a mind.

It's a disturbing proposition, that this library offers something everyday life can't offer, and so potent that everyday life attacks back. It would rip out the tongue of this library if it could. I've gotten lost here. I've mistaken the lives I've read about, the voices I've heard while reading. I read a novel, say, *One Day of Life,* Manlio Argueta, and the next morning, like this morning, I wake up and see as Lupe saw, waking at 5 AM in rural El Salvador, and I lie in bed listening to the birds Lupe describes. Oooops. Excuse me. Not "*Lupe* describes," *he,* Manlio Argueta, describes. I think.

But when I wake up like that the very day I awaken into, the very bed I wake up in, the birds I do hear right here, my wife in bed beside me, all that cries to mingle with the experience with Lupe, demands my attention to them even though they know they are Lupe and not-Lupe, even though they know I would choose them over this library if it came to a choice, even so they cry out in a kind of jealousy and I hear them, slightly ashamed.

The birds sing when I wake up but equally the bed squeaks and my back aches and I know we need a new bed and that it will cost such and such, and then I begin to wonder about whether we can afford it now or will have to wait and that takes me to thoughts about my work and what I'll be doing today and will I be doing enough to make enough money. Shouldn't I be doing more? Well, yes, maybe, but I can't sacrifice my whole life to earning money, can I? At the same time I can't just be a Don Quixote reading all the time. I'm no Don Thomas, but just Thomas Rivka, a real man. Why have I been lying in bed imagining Lupe outside San Salvador when I have to get up and get to work?

Then Marta wakes up. She wants to talk. We joke around a little. She's often amused when she gets up. Her mood balances mine. You see, I'm already far from the birds outside my window and those in my reading.

And the birds outside our window made an impression I won't think about all day. I won't think about them until I hear them again. But I will think about Lupe's birds. Why? And I can see why my birds are jealous of birds in a book which have nothing to recommend them, really. They're just black marks, scrawls, not even symbols, not even signs, just marks, dots.

When I talk with friends about our lives, or when I talk with Marta about her life, or my life, or our life together, it doesn't come close to when Marta, say, will tell me: "Thomas, I've been reading this book and it's wonderful. She has a whole dialogue in here between a man and a woman, it's a chapter which is really about death. It's the most unsentimental expression of love. I've read it over and over for the last few days." I'll go right to that book. When I read it, it means more to me about Marta than anything she might have told me from the day of her life, even had she told me some secret of her soul she'd been unable to talk about for twenty years. If what she told me were the darkest secret of her life, what she read and loved is the lightning which illuminates it.

Can I blame everyday life its jealousy? Sometimes, it seems, I'm its ally, and take its side against the library. Yet, I work to preserve this library. If we didn't work at it everyday life would win very quickly. It's a more powerful force with its winds, acids, waters, times, gravities, entropies, shifting lights, and us in the middle with what? with our reading.

Does that answer your question, Jake W.? I'll see you soon, when you get here.

all best

Thomas

VI / A Phenomenology of Change

Something momentous happens—the death of his father, a revolution somewhere he cares about, a serious fight with a good friend or with his wife, the fall of governments. And then, after a preoccupied absence of several days, or months, or even a year, Thomas will come back to the library. He'll be at the desk in the sunlight and it will astound him that the books all sit there as before, but now silenced by the supremacy of the events that shook Thomas's life, maybe the world's life. It occurs to Thomas, it *has* to occur to him, that without his intervention the books are dead.

He sits at the foot of the dead library of Thomas Rivka. He wants to insist that the books have an internal nervous system that language syntax rhythm nuance hyperbole metaphor metonymy lie distortion symbol sign system parole that he, Thomas, that he is not essential. That he is perhaps vital, all right, that he is one among many such vital components. But one among many.

Speak, he says to the library.

After the changes, pronounce. Recirculate. Accommodate to the revolutions. Go on like a human being goes on. Like history does.

Thomas refuses to get up from the desk, refuses to open a book and read it. He wants the library to make the first move, not to come to him necessarily, but to ignite itself. Perhaps all meanings of all words are changed. Regenerate, he seems to demand of the library. Move to the next level of being. Is it only me, he asks of his stone library, who has to make these leaps through hoops of descent? Don't the objects of our world come with us? Don't they have an *elan* of their own? a breath?

The library seems to be breathing. Is it because Thomas breathes, brought into breath by the very things he pursues in the library? Is it because he wants to imagine that it breathes? The books *want* to be read to be saved from suffocating stasis. Begin again. Somewhere in fiction.

VII / An Alphabet of Desire

Words that want to be objects

then discontent (self-conscious) with the objects they become (words) they depend on Thomas, their reader, undoubting Thomas, for a life's blood.

But if words "depend" then no discourse among them

so they don't depend even on Thomas?

That's yet another reason why, Thomas had to realize, he built his library on the line of infinity. Wasn't his own spine designed on the same axis? What happened then when mankind, evolving, stood up then looked out

Thomas climbed to the top of the stairs and felt the railing all along the open side of the stairway as though it were his spine. Spinal cord, cauda equina, spinal nerves: posterior horn, anterior horn, spinal meninges, afferent nerve, ganglion, synapse, efferent nerve. Codex of messages. For example: the spinal nerves consist of hundreds of thousands of individual nerve fibers. These include motor fibers from motor nerve cells in the cord destined for the skeletal musculature, as well as sensory nerve fibers from peripheral sense organs. The thin layer of connective tissue on the surface of the nerves carries small blood vessels. All this travels into the brain stem, medulla oblongata, and radiates throughout the arbor vitae, the cerebellum, the cerebral meninges, cerebrum, corpus callosum, pineal body, third ventricle, corpora quadrigemina, hypothalamus, pituitary, fourth ventricle, pons. Connected to the optic nerve. Reading.

The handrail, like the bookshelves, is local oak, harvested at about 60 years of age, spore, ring, bark, artery, branch, leaf. The tree is cut, planed, sanded, sawed, bundled, shipped, measured, cut, sanded, sealed with a new liquid into its pores. The handrail is rounded, like a spinal cord, so that when Thomas rubs his hand over it he can imagine that it is a spinal cord, a system, a bloodflow, an arbor vitae. And that only in the act of reading does a certain kind of meaning? Or intelligence? Or emotion?

When he got to the top Thomas looked out the round window inset into the wall. As he gazed boundaries were dissolving. The window dissolved into the wall, the wall and the library behind him dissolved into each other, yet when he turned around he saw the clear shape of the library, intact, all those books, all that language contained? uncontained? traveling? radiant? silent? speechless? dependent? free?

*

words that want to be objects

then content with the objects they become (words), vegetative, absorb *elan vital* like sponges, expand into the density of a page, include their origins, their antonyms, future meanings, agitate, fill your eyes

*

or that zero is a practical invention, like the passive verb. That it doesn't exist? What is that point, then, where the wall meets the floor? A fiction? There is no such point? The point is a moving point? A point made up of the predictive possibility of points? An imaginary, but necessary point? A point only imaginary but necessary for us to imagine? But why imagine it? Because imaginable?

If I were to stretch out my arms along the same configuration as the wall, left arm descending through zero, right arm ascending, zero would be at the heart. How strange. But that's mere metaphor and interpretation. The fact is the heart pumping blood down through the left up through the right arm muscle tissue viscera nerve cell dermis epidermis. There is no zero point on the body though we imagine one all the time: in the mind (even identifying it somewhere in the rear of the cortex, above, near the top, a point of floating zero), in the sex, in the heart, just above the pubis and just below the belly. Have we imagined zero in mathematics because first we chased it through the body and could articulate it only in mathematics? Then the mathematical zero itself is a metaphor.

but the point (or imaginary point) on the floor from where the wall of the library rises is not a metaphor. There must even be some nail there anchoring the wall. Or just above zero. It must be too thin there for an actual nail. Zero is too thin for an actual nail. And I am too human to stop making metaphor, to stop making meaning which may obfuscate meaning.

Zero is practical because you can't do decimal—or the calculations of any system—without zero.

Prior to the invention of zero the Babylonians used positional arithmetic to solve problems, but the method was confusing.

The Hindus must have had a zero digit before Christ, but there is no record of it prior to the 9th Century. (Saying 9th counting the centuries *since* zero)

Why did Thomas build a library based on infinity, based on zero? Because, he reasoned, just as in language, where infinitely many words can be composed of but a small variety of different characters, so also in arithmetic are numbers, infinitely many of them, composed of but a small variety of numerals. The devising of a scheme whereby an infinitude of things can be represented by means of a small number of symbols, and where the whole scheme itself is based on a symbol representing no-thing, must be among the most far-fetched achievements of the human intellect, and without it an advanced development of either language or arithmetic is unimaginable. And that's hard to conceive, without language or arithmetic to conceive with.

That's the beginning of the human intellect. It's a beginning that passes through the zero of history: prior to that zero there is no arithmetic and so no real language. After that zero there is everything in time. Where in history exactly is that zero? Where in time? Where in the body? When does it begin in the body? Is it carried in the sperm? Ova? One or two zeros?

Everything, even this library, built on a fiction. Yet pick up a book, begin reading. Franz Fanon's *The Wretched of the Earth*. Out of zero life ferments like some brew. Narrative, persona, events rise out of some zero point and we know that each narrative discusses also the re-descent through that zero point through which it has passed to become visible.

Thomas speculates that he should name the library "Zero." Rather, he thinks, were he to name it he'd have to name it some more concrete word which comes after zero. What, for example? he asks himself.

VIII / The Desire of an Alphabet

...came to the library and began reading one I've read and re-read, *The Myth of Sisyphus*. Then what happened? The letters began to rise, fly like they were running to escape the page even to escape their configuration as words. The whole book was a mess. I couldn't disentangle a thing from it. The letters couldn't get far, I supposed, because they are really very small things, each one of them. They're not very sophisticated in the ways of nature or mechanics. They have a limited range of experience, even if that range within itself is immense. So they didn't get far, the letters. They huffed, they breathed hard. They seemed gleeful to be free of the words that held them. Most of them lay on the floor exhausted. Some were laughing but I couldn't tell if their laughter wasn't demonic, a laughter of denigration. Some of the letters stretched as if to change into different entities, whether that be letters or some other object. Where was the author in all this? I thought about him as though his name were some sort of conjuring stone that would realign everything into what it had been aligned by him in 1942 in France. Somehow it seemed that the force of his intelligence, Albert Camus's culture knowledge historical incidence language personal psychology all played a critical role in distinguishing this book from the chaos or the non-existence that had preceded it. Albert Camus. As though I could rearrange all this as though I could be Albert Camus.

But I didn't want to write *The Myth of Sisyphus*, I wanted to read it. Maybe because I'm tired of the burden of myself and I want to subsume myself in something other than myself and I call that something other. Did the letters fly off specifically because they caught me in that kind of self deception?

What does that mean, "deception"? There's a good notion. Take a look at the word. Rescue letters from the chaos of Camus's debacle. d-e-c-e-p-t-i-o-n. They seem to weep when I pick them up. Why? Have they suffered? Isn't this what they wanted, to be liberated? dee eee cee eee pee tee eye oh ehn. I tried to read a certain history in each letter, to discover what word it had come from, but nothing told that. There was no trace of ancestry, as if each letter were an absolutely free and new thing, unlike myself, unlike anything else that I knew of or could think of. Unless you crossed what it then became absolutely clear was another boundary of a qualitatively different kind: you looked at the letter as a mere object, as ink. Then it had a history. But that boundary seemed ineradicable. Once the letter became a letter its history as plant, as pigment, as ink resolved by a leap into a letter from which perhaps it could further resolve forward but not backward, as if a leap itself of whatever kind is extra-natural and so ineradicable. And yet, as a letter which had been used in at least one previous and important word in an important book, it had no trace of any history beyond the fact that the dee couldn't be used in place of an eff. Like an infant I put the letter dee into my mouth to see what I could learn from it. It was tiny, not rigid, but solid. It tasted like a root, a potato or leek or rutabaga. It tasted of trace elements.

I asked Camus about the whole mess. What I wrote had meaning and importance, he said. I meant for it to be understood. I didn't write it so it would rupture into a million shards of chaos. I certainly understand ambiguity. I know about language's penchant for lying. I'm a practical man. I never denied metaphysics but I had to talk about what we could use. I don't know what caused the pressure inside the cohesion of these letters to explode. I don't know what caused the coherence to fail. I gave it everything.

Now I felt guilty. Did I have something to do with this infernal disintegration? My lack of respect for the book? My ordinary anger? My lack of insight or understanding? My hostility toward the truth of the ideas in the book? Maybe I was just at the end of my rope. Maybe I was just tired of the abysmal rock falling. Then my guilt disintegrated in reason, as Camus predicted that it would. How can I be so self-centered, once again, to think I caused this upheaval? These books have lives of their own.

I shuffled what was left of the letters of the word "deception" back into the pile. I walked out of the library leaving the letters scattered in a mess all over the place, on the stairs, on the desk. I didn't know what to do, except to sweep them up into a box of some kind, and buy another copy of the book. I loved that book ever since I first read it on my sixteenth birthday and it thrilled me.

I had notes written in a teenager's hand. Can I find them in this mess? All I can do now is make this record of what happened and rest, because I'm exhausted, as the letters seemed to be, exhausted from coherence and restless in chaos.

IX / *The Means of an Alphabet*

...and then Thomas spent a good deal of time trying to discern whether those exact letters from *The Myth of Sisyphus* wouldn't form some other book—not a book waiting to be written, because that would involve an unrealizable infinitude of possibilities, but in fact some other well known book already written. He considered other books of about the same size, Cerot's *de Mathematiques,* Mann's *Death in Venice,* Gertrude Stein's *Cities of Cities,* Jean Yves Collette's *The Death of André Breton.* It was an enormous task even to consider these very limited possibilities. After a little work Thomas had to give it up. Albert Camus's relationship with Thomas Mann or with Gertrude Stein or with Herman Melville was insignificant as some letter for letter correspondence, astonishing as that might be were it true. But it would only be a miracle, and miracles reveal so very little.

Thomas commissioned the building of a box to contain the letters of his *Myth of Sisyphus.* There were twenty-two thousand three hundred forty nine letters left. Thomas counted them in a new edition he bought. He felt ridiculous sitting on the top stair of the library beneath the window obsessed with the exact number of letters in a book only forty-eight years old—not old at all, hardly read, barely understood. Thomas recorded the number of letters in the back of the newly bought edition, and considered how some future owner of this volume might try to understand why anyone would have gone to the trouble of counting the letters in this book. What could anyone learn from that? Then that subsequent reader, that future owner of the book (an unrealized persona Thomas often considered, and considered that there might be a string of such characters stretching out into a fairly distant future) might meditate on that figure: 22,249. They might say it over and over to themselves, trying to find or to lose some meaning in it: twenty-two thousand two hundred forty nine, twenty-two thousand two hundred forty nine, twenty-two thousand two hundred forty-nine, twenty-two thousand two hundred forty nine, twenty-two thousand two hundred forty nine.

Thomas hired a cabinetmaker, a man whose son had done the carpentry work on the initial library. After eight months the father delivered a box made of African zebrawood, jointed to a Brazilian mahogany, interspersed with strips that had a hint of a local blond oak. On the lid he'd carved his own rendition of Sisyphus, loincloth clad, muscular, impressive. When the old cabinetmaker brought the box Thomas pulled out a bottle of Lephroig and together they sipped the smoky whiskey for two hours in the sunny part of the library away from the stairs, while they talked about Sisyphus, about the French, about the Scotch and their Scotch whiskies, about the box. Thomas talked about the workmanship involved in the carving, in laying in the hinges, in the intricate joints, in the lining. They talked about Thomas's wife, about whom the old man said, when they'd had four glasses each, that she was one of those women God put on earth to make other people realize that life after all was worth living. Thomas laughed because at that very moment his wife, exhausted from several weeks of overwork and excessive worry about problems with her work, lay inert and almost speechless in the den of their house, staring at the ceiling, trying not to yield to depression, but to rest, and regain her momentum.

By the time they had gotten well into the bottle of Lephroig the father was telling Thomas how absolutely the box was wrong. The portrait of Sisyphus was ridiculous. There was heroism, but no despair in his shoulders. There was no resignation in the wood. There was no good humor. The box was elegant. The wood was purposefully foreign and exotic. The dark blue lining was ostentatious. The box made not a sound opening or closing. Thomas walked with him out to his truck and the father, starting up the engine, sat for a while sunk into some thought. For a moment life seemed so unreal that the only reliable thing on earth was the hum of this engine as he felt it through his hands on the steering wheel. He didn't know if it was shame or whiskey that made him feel so insubstantial, though whiskey had never done that before. He didn't know who he was. When he looked up at Thomas, he knew exactly who he was, because Thomas's face just then seemed to reflect like a mirror exactly what the old fellow thought and felt. He said to Thomas, "it takes some of us so long to learn such obvious things that it's clear we'll never really learn them."

Thomas led the father, too drunk to drive, out of the cab of the truck, and put him to bed upstairs. He cleared out the bottle of Lephroig and the whiskey glasses and the ice bucket. He lay on the couch to imagine the best way to store those utterly errant letters, or if it was even important to do that. He could have used them to spell the old man's name, which was also Thomas, many times over, but he knew that he'd just be spelling his own name, and certainly that wasn't the reason the letters had disarrayed themselves, so that Thomas might use them to spell his very name like some obsessive chant.

The letters took on many qualities, one after another. For a moment, holding their shape, they seemed transparent. Thomas saw through them to the surfaces where they lay. In the next moment they seemed to stretch out to the very limit of their shape, so that an *s* stretched upwards and outwards in both directions until it was nearly not an *s*, but still barely discernible as an *s*, and stayed there for a moment, lingered on that edge of its definition, then slowly receded from the boundaries to the center of its *s*-ness. An *r* stretched out in the same way and then went past that boundary of definition, and disappeared. Colors rippled through them. In the next moment the letters seemed to be searching for each other, an *m* for a *p*, another *m* for an *a*, and so on, but soon that rattling stopped and they seemed still again. And as still, inert letters in fact they seemed most interesting. Thomas arranged a few letters into a few basic languages: c-a-t. c-h-a-t. e-c-h-a-d. n-o. They were still Camus's words, because Thomas was writing not what Camus would write, but what Thomas would write were he Camus, which he wasn't. Then he became more interested in the relationship between Albert Camus and Thomas Rivka than in the relationship between Albert Camus and Gertrude Stein. Thomas reached for all the letters and drew the huge pile toward himself. He rubbed the letters over his skin. He fashioned a few short words and as he spoke them pretended that they actually came out of his mouth strung together. He saw for the first time what the words that he spoke looked like, and though he thought the most interesting to see would be those abstract words which had only some thin referent in the world, such as ontogeny, such as responsibility, such as ordinary, but in fact the most interesting to see were those that were most specific, like horse, like hand, like pencil.

It became clear after not very much time at all that the letters needed no box, not even a simple one. They settled themselves at random around the library and it seemed they most indigenously belonged there, in among the books, lying in the desk drawers, kicked out to corners of the room, scattered up and down the particular line of that library's particular wall.

X / The Inclusion of Space

Bored, Thomas sat at the desk. He looked over the library, unable to imagine a book that might interest him. He took up a pencil from the desk. He drew small circles until they covered the page. He put down the pencil. He picked up a book from the desk. *The Posthumous Poet: A Suite for Pier Paolo Pasolini.* Pasquale Verdicchio. 1993. It was the last book he'd read. Out the large window he saw a huge airplane that must have been a DC10 or a 747 fall in a long, nearly meandering descent. It hit the ground at least seven or eight miles away but Thomas heard the sound of the crash. He picked up his pencil and began to scribble on another blank page. This time he filled it with triangles.

When the mailman came to the door Khlum barked like she does always at people who come to the house in uniform. The mailman wanted to talk about the plane crash, but Thomas just signed the receipt for the package the mail had brought.

Unwrapping it, Thomas found the complete 6 volume set of Bartolomè de las Casas's *History of the Indies.* There was a letter from one Señor Rudolfo Tapia, from the town of Miguelita, Michoacan, Mexico. The letter read:

Dear Mr. Rivka,

I have read in our local newspaper about the experiences you have in your library. I am fascinated by the events our reporter described occurring to you on December the 31st last, when you went to your library haunted by a dream of a violence to which you could not respond, and seeking for the vigor of the "honest fury of the outright imperialist conqueror Cortes." You are of course correct in assessing that quasi-madman's romp through Mexico. Since you are a Norteamericano, I wanted to point out that you have—if you so need it—a predecessor closer to your national heart than Cortes.

Your own Christopher Columbus—who never set foot on your actual land, but whom you claim as your founding discoverer—was the equal of Cortes in any match for brutality, and if you wish to invoke gods—even if it is a god of blood and brutality you wish to invoke—I find it is always strongest to invoke one who already has at least a mythical presence in one's own locale. As in Norteamerica you celebrate Columbus, I thought it meet that you should have these volumes of Columbus's biographer, and my personal hero of the Conquest, Bartolomè de las Casas. Despite my researches, I will never be able to know who was the more extreme idealist and romantic dreamer or who the greater realist? Was it Columbus? Or Sr. de las Casas?

As I said, I am fascinated to read of the accounts of your work in the library. As our village is small, our local newspaper uses such accounts only to fill in when there is a need to do so. There is no predicting when an article on your work may appear. That is better. Each day I buy the newspaper just before lunch at about 2:00 in the afternoon, with the expectation that I might read more about your fascinating explorations.

I hope these volumes of de las Casas find a proper place in your library. Moreover, I hope you find them as illuminating as I have.

Please forgive any distractions in my English writing from the norm. I am not a native speaker of your language, although I have labored at it carefully during my years of study abroad.

Very sincerely yours,

Sr. Rudolfo Tapia

Thomas opened Volume III of the tomes to page 356 and read:

Marriage laws are non-existent: men and women alike choose their mates and leave them as they please, without offense, jealousy or anger. They multiply in great abundance; pregnant women work to the last minute and give birth almost painlessly; up the next day, they bathe in the river and are as clean and healthy as before giving birth. If they

> tire of their men, they give themselves abortions with herbs that force stillbirths, covering their shameful parts with leaves of cotton cloth; although on the whole, Indian men and women look upon total nakedness with as much casualness as we look upon a man's head or at his hands.

The air filled with the shrill sounds of hundreds of sirens. Thomas took the package back into the library and re-read the paragraph again. He turned the pages:

> Endless testimonies...prove the mild and pacific temperament of the natives...But our work was to exasperate, ravage, kill, mangle and destroy; small wonder, then, if they tried to kill one of us now and then...The admiral, it is true, was blind as those who came after him, and he was so anxious to please the King that he committed irreparable crimes against the Indians....

Thomas took the pages scribbled with circles and triangles all over them, turned them over, and began taking notes. He worked for several hours, going back and forth between the various volumes Sr. Tapia had sent to him. He finally came upon this paragraph about slavery among the Native Americans:

> Thus husbands and wives were together only once every eight or ten months and when they met they were so exhausted and depressed on both

> sides...they ceased to procreate. As for the newly born, they died early because their mothers, overworked and famished, had no milk to nurse them, and for this reason, while I was in Cuba, 7000 children died in three months. Some mothers even drowned their babies from sheer desperation...In this way, husbands died in the mines, wives died at work, and children died from lack of milk...and in a short time this land which was so great, so powerful and fertile...was depopulated...my eyes have seen these acts so foreign to human nature, and now I tremble as I write...

There were more explosions. What was not possible on earth? Thomas tried to imagine one thing that was not possible. Closed his eyes. The scent of gasoline/metal/plastic fires. Even the presence of someone like de las Casas was possible. Even to live in an age of boredom was possible. Even to live in an age where a box of books and an airplane from the sky arrive at almost the same moment was not impossible.

Now, as to this newspaper reporter. Could Sr. Tapia tell him who it was? No, the only way to find out was to go to Migueltia, Michuacan, Mexico. To rent a room in a hotel. To wait day after day, drinking coffee and eating *pan dulce* in the same cafe (it would be important to be each day in the same cafe) reading the newspaper, until an account of the library appeared. Then there would be a byline. He would go to the newspaper and ask to speak to the editor. He would stand at the desk inside the doorway until the editor came from an office in the rear. He would introduce himself. I am, he would say in his best Spanish, Thomas Rivka, from the United States, from northern California. He would pull the day's paper from under his arm, he would point to the article, and he would ask the editor to tell him, please, who is the journalist who has been writing these articles about the library of Thomas Rivka. The editor would pick up the phone, dial a number, talk too fast in Spanish for Thomas to understand, hang up the phone, and wait quietly. A woman would appear. She would be about five feet seven inches tall. She would have dark hair which she would wear pulled back into a bun. She would be wearing professional dress. She would speak only a little English. She would say that she had been writing the articles about the library of Thomas Rivka, and that she made them up entirely. She is sorry, she would say, but no such library actually exists. It was only filler for the newspaper. She would tell Thomas that she was the great-granddaughter of a New York journalist who did a similar thing at the New York Sun in the 1880s, that he had made up a series of articles about telescopic discoveries on the moon. Everyone believed him, it had been a great success. She meant no harm. Yes it does, it does exist, he would tell her. It does. That's why I've come here. To find you and to tell you that it does exist. I am Thomas Rivka.

When he would get back home Thomas would think to name the library the Bartolomè de las Casas Memorial Library or the Library de las Casas, not because de las Casas had had the courage to tell another truth in his volumes, but because he had written at one point that "I myself writing it as a knowledgeable eyewitness can hardly believe it..."

XI / The Construction of Time

6:43 AM

as exile where habitually uninhabitable the homelands we recreate bit by detail word by. Only in reading does, which also is departure to arrive at some beginning, not axis, nexus, neither here nor. Therefore. and because. Because to read is to establish in time a timeless event, reading breaks time. Each occurrence of reading is an event which occurs only once, but from then on continuously. Therefore reading, which transsuspends time, substantiates it. Because. And therefore. Therefore only in reading, which is also change, alter, alteration, denomination of the daily into the uniconographic irreligious metamorphosis back from the diurnal into the perpechoowum. Unless, that is, the scribbles of words which migrate into the scribblings of readings *are* icons, and then oh reading is iconographic; and unless, that is, perpetooum itself is in some way *spiritus* in which case reading is not irreligious altogether Oh no. No. I'm trying to establish a different meaning for the word "to read," the present participle, "reading," the past participle, "read," the adjective "readable," the noun "readability," a meaning closer to the origin (tracing the word back to its Anglo-Saxon root, *rædan,* from the earlier *rælhan,* which is cognate of the Anglo-Saxon [reflexive] form of *hlahan, to laugh)* of "to laugh to oneself."

Between the process of writing and the process of reading there is a vague border. I cross without papers or credentials. The guards, so lazy, are ill trained. The two practices of reading and writing, becoming arcane perhaps, must be of the same country. So that reading is departure. So that to read occupies the mind in a reverie of the object of its reading, distracts the mind from its preoccupations in order to make room for you to write—but you write without a pen, without inscription, uninscribedly (uninscribbledly?)—as you read, and nothing else can free you in exactly that way. Free mind, occupied. You don't write about what you're reading, but you write an unrealizable novel/poem in a spiral of revising drafts. It has no commercial prospects. It will never sell one copy. It has only one reader. A literary migration which takes into account the history of all literary invention. A perfection of form evolutionary. As complex or demanding as any one unanswerable riddle whose attempt to answer raises more, better puzzles, new novels reshuffling parts of the old. Nothing's discarded. And nothing's discarded. That's the Book you reader are now reading (yes, you, Thomas, I Thomas, am talking to you, Thomas) and only if what you read is internally strong enough to distract you from the Herculean strength of your daily pre-occupations can you get down to the real work of reading: the creation of your book: The Book of the Reading of Thomas Rivka. A history. A bildungsroman. A mystery. A psychological study. A picaresque. A commedia dell'arte. A farce. A nouvelle roman. A Biblos. An interior monologue which is a novel about interior monologue.

9:22 AM

had wondered about the dichotomy between action and contemplation.
the urge to dichotomize.
the intellectual instinct. the moment when the child looks into the mirror and distinguishes that they don't know who they are looking at and dichotomizes: points at her/himself: *who* is *that?*
the process of readings.
not harmonies, but neutralities.
not, but.
the structures of readings more than the structures of knowledges or of what is known.
there is only one character in these journals and I lose interest in him.
attempts to unite verb with noun, or subject with object, or time with the perception of time.
the baseball season is beginning.
things will change.
things will not change.

The library is arranged in an order which now makes sense to me. That order will have to change but not for a while. A heavy inertia lies in the effort. Having decided to discard certain books because I didn't like them or their authors, I can't forget them. They have a shadow existence on the shelves that I don't like, but that says something about the nature even of bad books. Maybe I should have kept only the bad books to argue constantly with them. That would create a text of a different order.

I understand the intentions of this library: not being medieval I don't look for a final *w* to take flight and us with it, or, of course god or gods; alack; or alas; the maze I create here is its own exit; the maze itself so corporal so incorporeal. Sor Juana Inez de la Cruz had the first great literary library in our Americas (to distinguish it from the great oral American libraries) so I think of calling it the Sor Juana Inez de la Cruz Library or the Sr Thomas de la Duda Creativa Library—

to distinguish it from the Cartesian Duda Destructiva. What library could ask itself "do I exist"? Every library knows so well that it eats, shits, fucks, sees, farts, has diseases like strokes where the body forgets itself, diverticulitis where the body inflames itself, peritonitis where the body eliminates itself, cancer where the body welcomes its enemy, immune deficiency where the body abandons itself in nakedness to its environment, or processes like parthenogensis where the body duplicates itself but with what must be some *différence,* metamorphoses where the body recognizes duration, or photosyntheses where the body absorbs the transformation of what we so intuitively call energy, or digestion where the body extracts and expels, or birth where the body tumbles through the body into the distance from the body and so on and so on. *cogito?*

So that even reading is not *cogito.* Oh Sor Juana de la Crossed Eyes Tired from Reading late and long past the mid and well into the waning night where you have a little peace from your enemies in which to think, pray, write or at least imagine that you write—for fear of the possible persecution attendant upon actual *scriptus,* dear Sore Juana tired of fighting them so reading for yourself and so writing for yourself even if unscribbled except in that perpetuum you kept going and now I keep going for you, your scribe, having traveled north a few thousand miles, northwest, and many years

2:15 PM

if dream is insufficient and therefore the library. or where in a life dream *becomes* insufficient and therefore was that concurrent with the moment of the mirror when it discovered itself and so invented more and therefore the library. Because the library does need (to contradict myself on this day (like all of them) of contradictions) the *cogito*—dream abandons, and reading requires it. Though the library does want to approach the ordering principle of the dream, because the library, in all of its eloquence, discourse and fragmentation recognizes its multiple refractions, and imagines it might partake of what it imagines to be the ingenious ordering of dream, that unpremeditated form of the discourse of image. The library certainly knows (and/or I certainly know) that that discourse, running off in all different directions, is what creates the spark that makes the library itself visible. I can read a book and then give the book to someone else to read. They, while reading, will be writing their own book. The library knows that reading is a glance off the mirror, and subsequent to dream.

And could it be that I have one book, and many mirrors?

No. There's no fooling yourself, Thomas, or reducing things to any minimums. This is the minimus/maximum, *sans différence*. Vous l'avez. Lo tienes. You, who speak to yourself as though you are an Other with an intelligence greater than that of yourself, whom you lecture. Or with whom you discourse, running back and forth among all your ideas and potentials. The library then is the record of my discourse? No.

The library is its own discourse. You listen in, don't you?

Yes.

You're an eavesdropper?

No. I sit in the middle.

In the middle of yourself, or of the Other?

Neither, of course. Sorry.

And what goes running off in a thousand directions never returns?

No. Its only return is its destination.
Its embarkation?
Yes.
Hence this library?
Therefore, etc.

4:45 PM

I'd thought of arranging the library in so many different ways. One of them was to put all the books together which relied more on content, and all the others together which relied more on form. I began to work on that, but ran into this problem: a recognition that form-and-content was another level of discourse, and my choices became a critical judgment of that discourse. Then to put all the books that carried on that discourse well in an ascending hierarchy according to my judgment, and all those books that failed that discourse in a descending hierarchy, seemed finally to achieve a form of organization which expressed a level of understanding.

A book of excellent reproductions of Titian couldn't be classified according to Titian's discourse between light and shape, but according to the way the book shaped, or revealed, or played ironically, or developed, or undercut, or discovered, or argued with, or claimed Titian's visions. I was approaching an organization which was itself a book. And about a year later I was coming to understand how organization is subject to entropy.

Then I wanted to go beneath the zero point on the floor from which the library's main wall rose. Not to the basement, of course, though that intrigued me for a while as the most literal rendering of the most abstract idea and so in itself a dialogue between form and content. For several years, imagining ways to go beyond the zero point, I arrived at the zero point, seemed for a time to revel in it, but have found no way yet to occupy it with a library because it's already occupied or it's already occupied with a library. Is it always true that we have to extend ourselves beyond our capacities and then be brought back, exhausted enough to accept a world as it is? The beginning of a new discourse, which seeks a new form.

8:30 PM

Terrible time. Wind through windows. Awful fears descents thinking of my talk today with B. so young cognizant of things. I feel for him. He wiggles for value or even better, beauty. I pull out a few rugs. He's asked me and he's very ready. Reveals vast ugliness. Sorry, B. I have some faith in you. Meanwhile he misinterprets his dream and by the time he gets it right where will I be? Such recognitions he'll have his mind wanders now from its moorings. Open the windows goddamn it! Some gestated fire in these winds. B. meets me in the library here with his own books that he's brought. We talk. He talks about his sister and about his father's obsessive religion. About C. About his reading. About Werther. Can't write now. Too much to do. Preparations for tomorrow.

now which day has been lived? my day or the day of my reading? or have I done because I have done what I read? or have I remembered that part of the reading because I have done that same act in my day? the lines are as unclear as they should be, yet dim, tempting. Reading and life: they bleed into each other and sometimes I fear because of it. Easy to lose oneself. Oneself wants to be lost? oh you. Horus lachrymus. Watches the day pass. Witness the desire of day passes. Oh my library. Simple word: liber but having nothing to do with liberty that release from bondage. This is an escape into bondage, n'est-ce pas? Still the desire for permanence? Even that sentence beginning with *still*. All day like M. Grand perfecting one sentence. And day. Because sun, moon. Who am Boetheus, perhaps, his comfort. What consolation? Think of the challenges; the many starknesses revealed, unassuaged; the agonies; the disappointments: Bloom sees Blazes; Cortes back to Spain; Ozymandius, Alexander's Egypt. Satan spies Eve. Even in those, especially in those: the art that accepts them and just by accepting them...

or is it possible that a library which begins at zero and ascends toward entropy nothing blue heaven doesn't actually exist—it supplants it only compensates for what leaves a hole in a human's heart and so it doesn't exist? Yet here, right here, Thomas, is right where you sigh your acceptance and begin with your alpha. *Once.* There. Yes. *Once upon time.* A day let go of where solitude replaces the fear of solitude first is remembered in its images—and that is a kind of *scriptus*. I'm astonished every time I realize the extent to which reading creates living. Or a verso vice versa? It comes. In a progression of moments you realize it. It takes the mind synapse for synapse with acts of conflation: some memory from reading you remember as your memory. Or some memory of reading. Or some actual memoire. Public libraries demand silence because there is *already* so much noise going on inside them, everyone, so sotto, voce, hundreds of voices, each one's hundreds of, voices, such a racket pandemonium in league now the melancholy hour has passed which is mega... melan ... yes *melas cholë* ah black bile ... madness ... well ... timeless, eternal—Plato's—madness at least into form from nothing into forms plural

3:03 AM

the rule of unity now, no? not yet. 6:43 AM not til then. the old Doctor.

well, there is someone who does read it, that book unscribbled unrecorded but being composed. some figure quite impassioned takes notes, refers to this library to study it, understands it only by references. My grandfather reminds me of he does young cobbler he wanting to be a scholar haunted the academes peasant someone like him haven't dreamt of him in eons long gone he now soured face smiling at me: not him quite not exactly but quite like I've drawn on him as a writer draws on real ones so the reader/silent-writer draws on one to create his own student/reader of his own silent work dreams of him gets up at 3:01 AM writes a few notes in the library then goes back to sleep beside the breathing body who hums some minor complaint she loves to hum at him at being woken from her work Freud called it or him bearded was? no rather my grandfather so clear dreaming of it now I'd search through the books wouldn't I looking for him for whom I see all this is done this library so that he will have a source-guide for the work I write which is the work he wanted to write or wrote perhaps in his own way tools in hand as it were I suppose images minutes fresh dimming dammnit as though they were something to hold to dimming into secrets I don't know but that I the silent/writer will draw on silentwriter sounds like a new computer sort aha the silentwriter by macintosh the man in the macintosh back to references and they a kind of dream no n'est-ce pas my love? n'est-ce pas?

THE NEW AMERICAN FICTION SERIES

1 *Wier & Pouce,* Steve Katz
2 *Mangled Hands,* Johnny Stanton
3 *New Jerusalem,* Len Jenkin
4 *City of Glass,* Paul Auster
5 *Ghosts,* Paul Auster
6 *The Locked Room,* Paul Auster
7 *Blown Away,* Ronald Sukenick
8 *The Memoirs of the Late Mr. Ashley,* Marianne Hauser
9 *Country Cousins,* Michael Brownstein
10 *Florry of Washington Heights,* Steve Katz
11 *Dread,* Robert Steiner
12 *Family Life,* Russell Banks
13 *Painted Turtle: Woman with Guitar,* Clarence Major
[now Sun & Moon Classics: 73]
14 *The Sea-Rabbit,* Wendy Walker
[now Sun & Moon Classics: 59]
15 *The Deep North,* Fanny Howe
[now Sun & Moon Classics: 15]
16 *Hotel Death and Other Tales,* John Perreault
17 *Music at the Evening of the World,* Michael Brownstein
18 *Metaphysics in the Midwest,* Curtis White
19 *The Red Adam,* Mark Mirsky
20 *A Free Man,* Lewis Warsh
21 *The Petrus Borel Stories,* Tom Ahern
22 *The Fortuneteller,* Mac Wellman
23 *Tar Beach,* Richard Elman
24 *The Harry and Sylvia Stories,* Welch Everman
25 *Price of Admission,* Sam Eisenstein
26 *The Crimson Bears, Part II,* Tom La Farge
27 *The Idea of Home,* Curtis White
28 *My Horse and Other Stories,* Stacey Levine
29 *Djbot Baghostus's Run,* Nathaniel Mackey
30 *Place of Shelter,* Nolan Dennett
31 *A Hundred Doors, The Crimson Bears, Part II,* Tom La Farge
32 *Crow Time,* Sheila Cudahy

33 *Swanny's Ways*, Steve Katz
34 *Annie Salem*, Mac Wellman
35 *Nemo*, Paul Vangelisti
36 *The Returns*, Dennis Barone
37 *Puddingstone*, Mark Mirsky
39 *Dra—*, Stacey Levine
40 *The Library of Thomas Rivka*, Martin Nakell
41 *The Catastrophe*, Robert Steiner